Disney Princess

Snow White

AND THE SEVEN DWARFS

A Big Surprise

Written by
Melissa Lagonegro

Illustrated by
Artful Doodlers

This book belongs to:

Disney Princess

Snow White

AND THE SEVEN DWARFS

A Big Surprise

Disney PRESS
Los Angeles • New York

Published by Disney Press, an imprint of Disney Book Group.

Originally published in *Snow White's Secret* by Random House Children's Books

For information address Disney Press, 1200 Grand Central Avenue, Glendale, California 91201.

ISBN 978-1-368-02803-5
FAC-023680-19152
Printed in China
First Box Set Edition, July 2018
3 5 7 9 10 8 6 4 2

For more Disney Press fun, visit www.disneybooks.com
This book was printed on paper created from a sustainable source.

Snow White and her prince had recently been married, and they were living happily at the castle. The Seven Dwarfs missed Snow White, but she made sure to visit them often.

One spring day, Snow White went to the Dwarfs' cottage. The Dwarfs were not expecting her, but the princess had a very special surprise planned for them.

Snow White knew the Dwarfs worked hard. That day, she wanted to make sure that when they got home, they wouldn't have to do any more work—no dusting, no sweeping, and no cooking.

Snow White waited until the Dwarfs had left. Then she and her animal friends hurried into the cottage.

The princess looked around. “By the time the Dwarfs get home tonight, our surprise will be ready.”

So they set to work. Snow White sang a cheerful song as she swept the cottage floor. The birds chirped while they picked up crumbs. The squirrels used their fluffy tails to dust. And the chipmunks and deer washed and dried the breakfast dishes. With so many helpers, Snow White had the downstairs gleaming in no time.

Next they went upstairs, and the princess began to make the beds.

"Pull the covers up tight," she told the bunnies. "Then fold down the top. There, it's perfect!"

The bunnies hopped off to start on the other beds.

Before long, every inch of the Dwarfs' cottage was neat and tidy. Snow White and the animals headed outside to gather fresh berries, nuts, and apples to use in the Dwarfs' supper.

"They'll be very hungry after their long day," said the princess. Luckily, the blueberry bushes had lots of ripe fruit, and the basket was quickly filled.

"I know what we'll make for dessert," Snow White told the rabbits. "Blueberry pie!"

Next the princess and her friends strolled into a meadow to find some wildflowers.

"Lovely!" said Snow White as she sniffed a blossom. "These will be perfect for the table."

Back inside the cottage, Snow White and her friends got to work fixing supper. There was soup to be simmered, bread to be made, and pie to be baked.

Before she knew it, the late-afternoon sun was casting long shadows across the windowpanes.

Tweet! Tweet! Chirp! Chirp!

A bluebird was singing outside the window. That was the signal to tell Snow White that the Dwarfs were almost home.

Snow White and the animals hurried outside and hid. She couldn't wait to see what the Dwarfs thought of their surprise.

She peeked in through a window.

When they got inside, the Dwarfs stopped and stared. They could not believe their eyes. The floors were swept, the room was tidy, and there was even a freshly baked pie cooling on a windowsill!

"What is that delicious smell?" Doc wondered.

"Look!" cried Grumpy. He pointed to the table, which had been set. Then he went to the pot of soup. "Someone's been in our house."

The Dwarfs were confused. They tried to guess which Dwarf had done all of this.

Doc noticed that Happy's smile was especially big. Was he keeping a secret? Dopey pointed out that Sneezy seemed super sneezy—maybe because he had dusted and swept the cottage?

Snow White giggled as she listened outside the window. "They'll never guess that we did it," she whispered to her animal friends.

When the Dwarfs started to eat their pie, Snow White quietly headed home.

Inside the cottage, Bashful had one more guess. Whoever was behind the surprise would have to be one tired dwarf! And who seemed the sleepiest? Why, Sleepy, of course!

The truth was, Sleepy wasn't the only one. After a long workday, their tummies pleasantly full, all seven dwarfs were ready for bed.

When they climbed the stairs, the Dwarfs found one last treat: seven neatly made beds and seven perfectly fluffed pillows.

As they drifted off to sleep, the Dwarfs decided to tell their good friend Snow White about this wonderful surprise the very next time they saw her.

“Remember, you’re the one
who can fill the
world with sunshine.”